The Philippines

The Philippine nation includes 7,107 islands, in three

main groups: Luzon, in the north, the Visayas in the

center, and Mindanao in the south.

❖

Less than 1,000 islands are inhabited. Two islands—

Luzon and Mindanao—together make up two-thirds

of the country.

❖

The nation's territory is more than 10,000 miles long,

but only 688 miles across.

❖

Kneeling Carabao and Dancing Giants

Celebrating Filipino Festivals

Text by Rena Krasno

Illustrated by Ileana C. Lee

Pacific View Press
Berkeley, California

S

To my beloved friend,
Carmen Segovia and her family

This book would not have been possible without the generous assistance of the following friends and associates: Jose M. Segovia, Carmen Segovia, Ligaya De Los Angeles, Cota Deles Yabut, Lenny Juarez of the Filipino Education Center, Jaime Veneracion, Dr. Cesar A. Majul, Suzanne Williams, Pam Zumwalt, Nancy Ippolito, Bob Schildgen, Terry Acebo Davis, Mark Ong, and Prima Ofril.

Contents

An Invitation

You're invited to a party. A party that everyone has been waiting for. There will be food and music and costumes. Does it sound like fun? You will be an honored guest. In the Philippines the party might last for days and draw people from miles around, or from all over the country. Do you like to fly kites? Sing songs? Watch a parade? Then you'll like these festivals. Want to come?

There's always something to celebrate somewhere in the Philippines. You couldn't go to every festival if you tried. There are too many! They honor famous battles, special animals, or holy days. There are festivals for water buffalo (**carabao**), Christmas, and the end of the Moslem holy month, Ramadan. There are races, contests, and dancing. Do you like food? Everyone cooks and everyone eats. There is even a night for taking food to the cemeteries to share with friends and family who have died.

There are 7,107 islands in the Philippines stretched between south China, Malaysia, Indonesia, and Borneo. Of these, 2,773 islands are so tiny they don't even have names. For thousands of years, these islands have been a meeting place for people from around the world. Ati, Indonesians, and Chinese from Asia, Arabs from the Middle East, Spanish and Portuguese from Europe all have walked or sailed to the Philippines. They all brought their own ideas, their own ways, and their own celebrations. No wonder there are so many festivals!

But don't expect copies of other people's parties. Filipinos wear masks and costumes, flowers and shells. They make music with gongs, drums, fiddles, guitars, and flutes. They have their own stories and their own history. Over the years, these festivals have become originals, made by Filipino people.

More than 70,000,000 people live in the Philippines today. They speak 87 different languages. Their main language, **Pilipino**, has 3,000,000 words, three times more than English! Most words come from **Tagalog**, which is spoken on the island of Luzon. Others come from Filipino dialects, from Chinese, Arabic, Spanish, and English. Filipinos are friendly, easy-going, fun-loving, and hospitable. They always make strangers feel welcome and invite them to every celebration.

Even the weather, plants, and animals in the Philippines make the celebrations special. It never snows in the Philippines. The rainy season goes from June to November. It brings strong storms called typhoons. Roofs blow off. Rain pours down in powerful streams. Streets quickly flood. All traffic stops. In the fields, crops are destroyed. People sometimes cannot protect themselves, and get killed. From December to February it is cool and dry. The weather becomes very hot and humid between March and May.

Thousands of kinds of plants, animals, and fish live here. The islands are the home of the Monkey Eating Eagle, the Cloud Rat, the Mouse Deer, the tiniest fish in the world, and many other strange creatures.

But the greatest treasure of the Philippines is the people. People who honor their past, celebrate the present, and look hopefully to the future. Whether they live in the Philippines, in the United States, in Canada, Hong Kong, or around the world, Filipinos have something to celebrate. You're invited. Come to the party!

Original Filipinos

Who were the first Filipinos? How did they get to the islands? What did they look like? What kind of place did they find when they arrived? In 1962, Dr. Robert Fox discovered the fossilized skull of a male pygmy (small person) in a cave on the island Palawan. Scientific tests proved the skeleton was about 25,000 years old. Surely this man was one of the first Filipinos.

Where could he have come from? It was the Ice Age. Much of the sea water was frozen at the earth's poles and the sea was lower than it is now, even in the tropics. At that time, the Philippine Islands were connected by land. They were joined to Asia by land bridges. Pygmies could walk from the Malay Peninsula, Borneo, and Australia to land that would later become islands. When the icecaps began to melt, the land bridges were covered with water, leaving the surviving pygmies on islands; 40,000 of their descendants, called **Ati or Aeta,** live in the Philippines today. Some live like they did thousands of years ago. Their main tool, a spear, is so important to them that they have 100 different names and uses for it.

The Ati had found a land rich in plants and animals. They fished, hunted, and later grew plants for food. There were many animals in the islands: crocodiles, wild pigs, squirrels, anteaters, porcupines, and wild buffalo.

Malakas and Maganda

The First Filipino People

Utang na loob (debt from within) describes an attitude of obligation and respectfulness. It is very important in the Philippines. Children offer their parents utang na loob for giving them life and bringing them up. They are expected to obey their father and mother and take care of them when they get old. All Filipinos must also be thankful to relatives, friends, neighbors, and others for any favors, big or small. It is a fine compliment to say about someone: "That person has utang na loob."

After the creation of the earth thousands of years ago, there was the land and sea, and there were plants and animals. But there were no people.

One day, the King of the Birds decided to leave his nest high on a cliff to see the wonders of the world. He flew for many hours. When his wings grew tired he rested in a big bamboo tree. Suddenly he heard a muffled sound coming from inside the tree.

"Oh great bird, free me! Free me please!"

The King of the Birds was so hungry he hardly listened. His eyes followed a fat lizard slithering down the tree. He tried to catch it but missed. Desperate for food, he pecked again. Tak! Tak! Tak! He caught the lizard and at the same instant split open the bamboo tree. Out sprang a handsome young man.

"You saved me, oh King of the Birds!" he said. "I am Malakas, the Strong One. I have been imprisoned for a long time in this tree. My mate, Maganda, the Beautiful One, is just below me. Please release her too."

The King of the Birds agreed. He gave another mighty peck. The bottom of the trunk broke in two and a beautiful maiden stepped out.

"Climb on my back," the King of the Birds told them. "I will fly you around the world and we'll choose the loveliest spot for your home."

Malakas and Maganda did as they were told. They clung to the King of the Birds' feathers as he soared higher and higher. They didn't let go even when strong winds blew and rains poured down.

After days of flying, the King of the Birds said, "Here we are at last!"

Malakas and Maganda looked down. Far below in the blue ocean was a string of islands like green jewels. As they flew closer, they saw trees heavy with fruit. Birds chirped and sang. Rainbow-colored butterflies fluttered. Fish swam in crystal-clear rivers.

Malakas and Maganda thanked the King of the Birds again and again. They begged him to stay and live with them in this enchanting land.

"We will always take care of you. We are so grateful. **Utang na loob**," said Malakas.

But the King of the Birds refused. "My world is high in the mountains and in the skies," he replied. "Your world is here in these islands."

He waved good-bye with his wings, then flew higher and higher until he became a tiny speck and disappeared.

Malakas and Maganda lived happily in their islands and had a big family. They were the first Filipino people.

Carabao

Star of the Farmers' Celebration

Ever since early Filipinos tamed the wild buffalo, farmers have worked with carabao.

The sun peeks over the fields. It is dawn. But farm children in the Province of Bulacan are already awake. Everyone is excited. Today is May 14th . . . the carabao festival. The big, friendly carabao (water buffalo) must be washed, the hair shaved off their bodies, and their hooves polished with oil. They must be beautiful for the parade honoring San Isidro Labrador, the patron saint of farmers. Every family hopes their carabao will be the most beautiful, the strongest, the fastest, or win the prize for the longest horns.

Now it is time to decorate the animals. Children drape garlands of flowers around the carabao's necks. They tie red, yellow, and green ribbons on their horns. They fasten fluffy tufts of straw around their feet and decorate their backs with bright fabric.

The children can hardly wait for the parade. Hundreds of carabao will march to the church. Some will pull carts carrying farmers' families, an image of San Isidro, flowers, fruits and vegetables, or seeds and tools. Streets will be crowded with people laughing, pointing at the animals and talking about them.

The carabao parade will end at the church. Some carabao are trained to crawl on their knees as they approach the church. Others kneel when they reach the church courtyard where a priest is ready to bless them and offer a prayer for a good harvest.

Family, friends, and neighbors have worked many days and nights fattening pigs, killing chickens, catching fish, chopping vegetables, and baking. The smells of coconut milk, spices, and roasting pork drift through the village. There will be enough food to last from early morning until late at night. Everyone, even strangers, will be welcome to share the meals and fun. After the parade the carabao can rest but the people will celebrate. They will sing, dance, eat, and play guitars all night. It is a special day for children, their families, and their carabao!

In the Philippines, the **carabao** is called *The Farmer's Best Friend.* In 1993, the Philippine government issued a postage stamp with its picture as the national animal of the Philippines.

9

Carabao
Philippine Water Buffalo

White egrets and black mynah birds ride on carabao working in the fields. The birds and the carabao both benefit. The birds watch for worms and insects the carabao uncover as they walk through the mud. They peck blood-sucking ticks from the carabao's ears and frighten away flies.

Even four-year-olds can care for the gentle carabao. Sometimes a carabao lowers its horns and lifts the child to its back or lets him climb up its leg like a ladder. The carabao recognizes every member of its Filipino family.

But the first carabao weren't friendly animals like these or the ones decorated for the Carabao Festival. They were wild buffalo. These frightening creatures could easily pierce people with their powerful horns. At first, Filipinos hunted them for their meat. Later, they tamed them and used them to plow and pull carts.

Today's carabao is a strong, gentle animal, perfect for working in muddy rice fields. While horses and oxen can only work on dry land, the carabao's broad hooves are good for wet earth. They stop the carabao from slipping and falling.

Carabao need to bathe every two hours when they work in the fields. Their leathery skin gets hot in the sun and they don't have sweat glands . . . except in their noses. Luckily, they are skilled swimmers. Filipinos sometimes call them "carabao fish." They can keep their heads under water for more than two minutes at a time, and eat submerged grass even during floods. Country people use the water-loving carabao to cross rivers standing or crouching on their backs. The carabao gets wet but the people stay dry.

A mother carabao takes good care of her calves. If her calf is attacked by a crocodile, she jumps into the water and defends him fiercely. She usually wins the battle and kills the crocodile with her horns.

Filipinos eat carabao meat and drink carabao milk poured over sliced fruit and crispy rice. They use fat-rich carabao milk to make ice cream and cheese. Children love carabao milk **pastillas**—a kind of toffee fudge candy flavored with lime or purple yam. The pastillas are wrapped in colored tissue paper cut into intricate designs of flowers, leaves, huts, harps, and letters.

Coconut Cookies

You can try this recipe for a special celebration.

1 cup butter
1/2 cup of any hard grated cheese
1 cup sugar
pinch of salt
1 teaspoon vanilla essence
1 egg
2 tablespoons milk
2 cups flour
1/2 cup grated coconut

Mix butter, cheese, sugar, salt, and vanilla. Add egg and milk. Beat well with hand or electric mixer until smooth and creamy. Add flour. Stir. Add coconut. Stir.

Take a non-stick baking sheet. Do **not** grease. Drop spoonful by spoonful of mixture on pan. Heat oven at 325 degrees. Bake about 20 minutes.

This should make about 50 cookies.

Sipa—A Filipino Game You Can Play

Do you like to play soccer? Have you ever kicked a rock or a pine cone down the street? Then you'll know why children in the Philippines love playing **sipa**. Children jump, hit, and kick the sipa shuttle. They look like they are doing a wild dance. During festivals, boys and girls show off their skills at playing sipa.

The point of the game is to kick a shuttle or ball in the air and not to let it drop on the ground. You may *not* use your hands, only your foot or leg. Each time you hit the shuttle you score a point. Some players are so good they score 100 points or more!

In the Philippines, many children make sipa shuttles out of paper or leaves. You can make your own sipa shuttle. You need a flat one-inch washer and strips of cellophane or wrapping paper. Fold the strips lengthwise, bunch them up, pull the folded part through the washer and leave the ends of the strips hanging free. These "bangs" make a flyer. The bushier the better!

Why the Carabao Has a Tight Black Skin

A Folk Tale

Hiya means shame. **Walang hiya** means without shame, shameless. In the Philippines, children are taught to be ashamed of themselves if they misbehave, or if neighbors, friends, and relatives think badly of them. A walang hiya person is someone who does not know how to act properly, who cannot tell the difference between right and wrong, who does not care what people say about him or her. To call a Filipino walang hiya is a big insult.

Filipino storytellers say long ago all animals wore clothes. At that time, a carabao dressed in a brown suit and a cow dressed in a black suit worked side by side on a farm. They plowed fields and dragged heavy carts from sunrise to sunset. A mean farmer owned them. He hit them with a thick stick whenever they stopped to rest, and never let them soak themselves in the cool river. The poor animals grew weaker and weaker and smellier and smellier. They knew they would soon die, and made plans to escape through a slit in the pen where the farmer locked them up every evening.

One night when there was no moon, the carabao and the cow pushed their thin bodies through the narrow opening and quietly crawled out. They ran as fast as they could to the river. Off went their sticky clothes and they dipped themselves again and again in the fresh water. Suddenly, they heard shouts in the distance. It was the farmer screaming in an angry voice:

"Where are you two? **Walang hiya** animals! Come back at once! If you don't, when I catch you, I will beat you until your backs bleed!"

Trembling with fright, the carabao and the cow climbed out of the river, got dressed, and began to run. They were so terrified they kept running even when they could no longer hear the farmer's cries. The cow went one way and the carabao another.

At dawn, the tired carabao bent down to drink from a pool. His clothes felt tight and uncomfortable. When he saw his reflection in the clear water, he realized he was NOT wearing his brown suit but the cow's black one! No wonder it was so tight. The cow was much smaller than he was.

Far away, the weary cow stopped to rest and thought: "I must be even thinner than before. My suit is too big for me!"

As the sun rose, she saw she was wearing the carabao's brown suit!

"Oh, we were in such a hurry we mixed up our clothes," she exclaimed. "We must change them when we meet!"

But they never saw each other again. That is why carabao have tight black skins and cows have loose brown ones.

Celebrating Rice

The Ati-Atihan Festival

*A legend says that the famous **Ati-Atihan** festival celebrates a gift of rice to **Ati** in ancient times. The Ati still live on an island south of Luzon in Aklan Province.*

How would you like to go to a party that lasts a whole week? The noise never stops. Drums bang, whistles blow, people bang on pots, pans, and coconuts. Strangers run through the streets smearing each other with soot, throwing buckets of water at each other, and yelling, **Hala Bira** . . . "Strike a blow!" You could paint your face, wear a wild costume, and sing and dance all night. But be careful! Some people blow tongues of fire from their mouths at the **Ati-Atihan** festival.

What are the people celebrating? The story says that long ago, the Ati, who are pygmy people and live high in the mountains, had planted rice. But rains flooded their crops and ruined the rice. They had nothing to eat. They were starving. The Ati left the mountains and went to the plains to look for food. Luckily, the crops in the lowlands had not been destroyed. The plains people shared their rice with the Ati and, the story goes, the Ati were so grateful and happy they danced for joy in the streets.

The plains people joined the fun. It must have been like one happy family. To make the dark-skinned Ati feel at home, the hosts rubbed soot on themselves. They made their skin the same color as the Ati's. Ati-Atihan means "pretending to be Ati." When Filipinos rub themselves with soot today, they are remembering that early celebration. The Ati people still come down from the mountains for the festival on the third Sunday in January. Local people and visitors throng to the celebration wearing masks and huge hats covered with feathers and beads.

If you and your family ever go to the Ati-Atihan festival don't be surprised if your parents or even your grandparents join in the yelling, jumping, and dancing. It's part of the celebration about early Filipinos who shared their rice . . . the celebration where, Filipinos say, "Even the streets dance."

Ati-Atihan ends after a procession enters the church and all noise and music stop. Then people walk together to the river and wash away all soot and dirt. They are now ready to return to everyday life.

Indonesians
Sailors, Rice Planters, and Engineers

The **Ifugao** believe that people must not fight nature but live with it. Their calendar has 12 seasons which they set by watching birds migrate, flowers bloom, and winds and rains change.

The Ice Age that allowed the Ati to walk over land bridges to get to the Philippines ended. The earth warmed, the seas rose, and the land bridges to Asia were submerged. The Philippines became islands. Now, only fearless sailors could reach them by sea; 5,000 to 6,000 years ago, Indonesians braved the crossing and settled in the Philippines. They farmed, mined, and made copper tools. Some historians believe Indonesians grew the first rice in the Philippines.

Later, Chinese, Malay, Indian, and Arab sailors landed in the Philippines, joining the Ati and the newer, taller, Indonesian settlers. Rice became the main food of the islands.

Ifugao tribes living in northern Luzon are descendants of Indonesians. In the local language, Ifugao means "eater of rice." Around 3,000 years ago, the Ifugao began to carve terraces in mountain slopes to plant rice. The terraces look like giant stairways to the sky. Every nook in the mountainside was transformed. There are so many terraces that, placed end to end, the paddies would go halfway round the world! The Ifugao had no machines. They used only spades and wooden stakes to make strong walls of earth and stone chips. Some of these walls are 75 feet high! Since rice needs so much water to grow, the Ifugao had to dig miles of ditches to bring water to the plants. Not one drop of water was ever wasted.

Keeping up the rice terraces was hard work. They had to pull weeds from between the stones so that the weeds would not break the walls apart. They always had to clear dirt, fallen plants, and dead animals from the irrigation ditches. They made repairs after earthquakes and storms. But their work paid off. The terraces of the Ifugao, the "rice eaters," have been used to grow rice for thousands of years, and are growing rice today.

Writing on Bamboo and Bark

Many Filipino tribes developed their own writing. Ancient Filipinos carved symbols on pieces of bark or bamboo. The Hanuoo-Mangyan people of Mindoro island still use their ancient script for poetry. This is an example of their ambanhan poetry.

Ka-wo-no-ma-ngam-bu-nam
Dag-am-bon-ya-mi-day-an
Pa-ngam-bon-ya-mi-ad-ngan
Ha-law-na-kan-mag-du-yan
Ha-law-pal-yo-yi-ma-an
Li-ba-yan-ta-la-yi-ban
Ba-ras-la-wod-A-nu-han

If you are angry with me,
don't be mad behind my back!
Face me and we can agree.
You know why I tell you this?
That I can go home in peace
To Libangan with the reeds,
where the Anuhan flood meets.

In the 16th century, the people who lived near Manila wrote the ancient Tagalog language with symbols that represented syllables. This writing is not used today, but some schools in the Philippines teach it in special classes. It looks like this:

How the Filipinos Discovered Rice

A Folk Tale from the Central Philippines

There are many words in the Philippines for rice. **Palay** is rice in the husk, **bigas** is raw rice, **kanin** is cooked rice, **tutung** is over-cooked rice which sticks to the pot, **malagkit** is sticky rice. Many Filipinos enjoy eating sticky rice wrapped in banana or coconut leaves and steamed.

A long time ago, a man named Siginhon and his wife, Tiginlan, settled on a small island in the Visayan Sea. They swam, fished, gathered roots and fruit and never went hungry. After some pleasant years, the weather began to change. The rains stopped, the plants and trees dried up, the rivers became muddy, and the fish died. It became harder and harder to find something to eat. Siginhon and Tiginlan were very worried, after their baby son was born.

"What shall we do?" cried Tiginlan in despair. "We will all surely die!"

"Don't worry," said Siginhon. "I will go and search for food."

He set off to explore the hills and valleys, but he didn't find any food. His last hope was the highest mountain on the island. Siginhon climbed its steep slope. Hours later he reached the top. Tall green grass he had never seen before grew near the summit. Siginhon noticed it had many little ears of grain. When he took one in his hand, he was startled to hear the plant say in a low crackling voice:

"May I help you? You look thin and hungry. My grains are delicious. Just shake off the husks and boil the grains in water. When they are soft and fluffy, you can eat them and grow strong again."

"Oh, thank you!" cried Siginhon. Without wasting any time he cut down a big bundle of grass, and rushed back home.

His family was waiting for him, impatient and hungry. The little boy looked sickly and was whimpering. Siginhon threw handfuls of grains into a pot and cooked them. Then they all ate a delicious meal.

Suddenly, they heard the grass speak. "Clear a plot of land and plant the rest of the seeds. The rains will soon start, the plants will grow, and you will never starve again."

Siginhon and Tiginlan planted the seeds. That night there were bursts of thunder, and rain fell. Soon jade-green grass sprouted from the seeds. It grew bigger and bigger until it swelled with grain. The little boy loved the long stalks that swayed in the wind and the white grains that made his favorite food. He was too little to speak but pointed at the grass babbling, "Pa-pa-pa! Ay-ay-ay! Pa-l-ay! Palay!"

Siginhon and Tiginlan heard him and decided to name the miraculous plant **palay** just like their son did. Palay is the Filipino name for the rice plant.

The Three Crystal Boxes

A Folk Tale

Rice is so popular throughout the Philippines that there are many folk tales about it. Here is another favorite story.

Pinipig was a little Filipino boy. One hot day he sat on a river bank after a rainstorm. A beautiful rainbow appeared in the sky. It started from an odd tree. This tree's branches were in the ground and its roots were in the air! Pinipig had never seen an upside-down tree before.

I'll climb this strange tree!" Pinipig thought and grasped its trunk. He climbed quickly up to the roots. In the distance, Pinipig saw a mysterious country.

"I must explore this new world!" he said to himself.

Most Filipinos eat rice at every meal, breakfast too! They even serve it at their late-morning and mid-afternoon snacks called **meriendas**. They especially like steamed or fried rice.

Off he jumped The air around him was violet, indigo, green, yellow, orange, and red. Strange plants and beautiful flowers bloomed everywhere.

A handsome young man in splendid silver clothes approached him.

"Welcome to Rainbow Kingdom," the stranger greeted Pinipig. "I am the king's son. Come and have dinner with me in my palace." Pinipig followed the prince to a magnificent crystal building. All the colors of the rainbow danced from its walls, floors, and roof. The prince offered Pinipig a bowl of fluffy white grain.

"What is this?" asked Pinipig with surprise.

"It is rice," replied the prince. "Our best food. We eat it morning, noon, and night." Pinipig tasted the rice. It was delicious.

"I will show you how it is grown," the prince told him. "If you stay here and learn, your village will never go hungry."

Pinipig was very happy. He knew how hard it was for his family, friends, and neighbors to find food.

After the meal, the prince took Pinipig to the rice fields. He taught him to sow rice, to plant it in rows, to give it plenty of water, and to protect it from insects, birds, and bad weather.

Pinipig stayed one whole year with the prince. Then he said to the prince, "You are my best friend but I am very homesick. I miss my parents, brothers, and sisters. They must be worried about me. Please, let me go home."

The prince was sad to hear this. He loved Pinipig and didn't want him to leave.

"I will miss you very much," he sighed, "but I know you must go to your family. Take these three crystal boxes. They are filled with grains of rice. Plant the rice from the round box at the beginning of the year, the rice from the square box during the rainy season, and the rice from the oval box in the dry season."

Pinipig thanked the prince. Then they walked together to the spot where the blue color of the rainbow began.

"Slide down," urged the prince, "you'll get back home."

Pinipig clasped his legs around the blue arch and down he went, sliding faster and faster, until he reached his village.

"Pinipig is back!" everyone shouted when they saw him. Pinipig told them about his adventures and showed them the grains of rice. He taught the farmers everything he had learned from the prince. Soon the country-side was covered with lush green fields. Everyone began to eat rice and it became the main food of the Philippines. They called pounded rice **pinipig**.

Song
Planting Rice

Nearly half of the farm land in the Philippines is used to grow rice. Rice planting is hard and tiring. Filipinos sing:

Planting rice is never fun
Bent from morn till the set of sun.
Cannot stand and cannot sit,
Cannot rest for a little bit.

Magtanim, hindi biro
Maghapong naka yuko
`di naman maka tayo
`di naman maka upo

Hari Raya Poasa

A Moslem Festival

Hari Raya Poasa is a celebration filled with food, presents, and candy for Moslem children in the southern Philippines. It is a joyful time at the end of a sacred month.

During the whole month of **Ramadan,** beginning with the new moon, all good Moslems fast (go without food). Only people who are too young, too old, or too sick are excused. The fast starts when you can tell a white thread from a black thread by the light of the moon. Food is served twice a day: a "night breakfast" before dawn and a supper at sundown. Between these two meals Moslems may not eat or drink anything at all, not even a drop of water! They must not smoke, think bad thoughts, or be rude or unkind.

Ramadan ends as a new moon appears, and the 10th month, **Shawal,** starts. The fasting stops and the Hari Raya Poasa Festival begins. It is a time to give thanks, a time for celebration and fun!

First, everybody helps clean the house. Children ask their parents to forgive them if they were naughty. Mothers beg fathers to pardon them if they did anything wrong. The fathers reply, "The same with me."

The whole family puts on their best clothes and prays at the **mosque,** the Moslems' temple. After prayers, children run to the town square. They have been waiting. They know what's coming. People throw handfuls of coins and candies up in the air. The children rush around grabbing what they can catch . . . a centavo, a peso, a special candy. They laugh and push and scream, scooping up goodies as soon as they land.

At home, women cook a huge feast. The whole community—friends, families, and religious leaders—may come together to celebrate. The table is full with banana, coconut, rice and wheat cakes. There are all kinds of pastries, mangoes, papayas, and vegetables. There is meat—usually chicken, goat, or mutton—and fish. (Moslems do not eat pork.) Food colored bright gold with spicy turmeric makes the meal glitter.

Later in the evening people gather outside to listen to religious leaders chant or recite verses from the Qur'an.

Moslems count their months by looking at the moon. The ninth month is called the **Ramadan.** Moslems believe this is when God, **Allah,** sent revelations, now collected as sacred writings called the Qur'an.

Arabs
Allah, Artists, and Musicians

It is easy to find shells in the Philippines. There are 20,000 species of shellfish there. The biggest one is a five-foot clam, large enough for a baby's bath!

More than 1,000 years ago Arab merchants sailed across the Indian Ocean and began to trade with the Filipinos. Arabs sailed from the Middle East bringing spices, silk, cotton, porcelain, and beads. The Filipinos sold them beeswax, amber, pearls, and coral.

The Arabs were Moslems. They taught the Filipinos their belief in one God, Allah. Soon, most Filipinos in Mindanao became Moslems. Today five out of every 100 Filipinos are Moslems. Their sacred writings, the Qur'an, and the Arabic alphabet are still taught in Mindanao schools.

If you go to Mindanao, the second largest island in the Philippines, you will see pictures of a royal bird, the **sarimanuk**. The sarimanuk looks like a peacock. It always clutches a fish in its beak or claws. Moslem Filipinos like to make pictures of the sarimanuk.

According to legend, **Sarimanuk** was the king's messenger. The king's son fell in love with a princess. He wanted to give her a precious engagement ring. As he strolled near a lake admiring the ring, he stumbled and dropped it into the water. A big fish swallowed it. At once, Sarimanuk plunged into the lake, caught the fish, and flew to deliver it to the prince's bride. Of course, she found the ring inside!

Moslem Filipinos are great artisans. They weave, carve wood, make beautiful jewelry, and brass pots. They like to decorate their work with shells.

Moslem Filipinos also make their own music and have their own instruments. The **kulintang** is a favorite Moslem instrument. It has a row of eight bronze gongs from large to small. The largest gong makes low notes. Each smaller gong makes a higher note. The kulintang is played with other musical instruments: a "timekeeper" gong, four hanging "talking" gongs, two "big" gongs and a drum. The musicians work as a team. They sit or stand very close to each other and take turns playing each instrument. The kulintang is only played for entertainment, healing, and communication. It is never played during religious celebrations.

Filipino Moslem women usually wear a wrap-around skirt called **malong.** It is a long piece of fabric worn with a body-fitting blouse. Women like to wear malong that are magenta, purple, pink, or green. The malong skirt can be used in other ways: as a cloak, a swimsuit, a blanket, a cradle to rock the baby, a hammock, a room divider, and even a burial shroud.

The Chieftain's Golden Heart

A Moslem Folk Tale

The mango is the national fruit of the Philippines. Filipinos eat mangoes fresh or make them into pickles, preserves, chutney (relish), or juice. Mangoes are used for salads, cakes, candy, and ice cream. They are rich in vitamins A, C and D.

There are lots of different mangoes in the Philippines: big **carabao** mangoes, smaller sharp-tipped **picos**, and a tiny soft mango from which people suck the juice after tearing a hole in its skin. Different mangoes taste sweet or sour. Some are smooth and some are more stringy.

In the large southern island of Mindanao, there lived a noble **datu** (chieftain) who had a beautiful daughter, Marang. From the time she was a little girl, Marang loved to visit the big market near the harbor. Merchants sold all kinds of wonderful wares there: silk, gems, china, food, and spices.

One day when she was 18, Marang went to the marketplace and spied a lustrous pearl necklace. She took it carefully in her hand and looked up at the dealer. He was a very handsome young man.

"What lovely pearls," murmured Marang. "They shine like moonrays."

"Please keep the necklace," said the vendor. "It's yours."

"Who are you? How can you give me such a lovely gift?" asked Marang with surprise.

"I am Ahmad," he replied. "My father is a chieftain in Arabia. I travel around the world to buy and sell beautiful things. Please honor me by accepting this necklace as a gift."

Marang smiled shyly, nodded, and Ahmad gently placed the pearls around her neck.

After that, every time Marang visited the market she stopped at Ahmad's stall to talk. Their friendship grew and soon they fell deeply in love.

At that time in Mindanao, parents chose husbands or wives for their children. One day, Marang's father, the datu, called her to him. "Marang," he said, "I will not live much longer. Before I die, I want to see you happily married. So, I have promised you, as a bride, to my best friend's son."

Marang dutifully bowed her head. How could she disappoint her beloved father by telling him about Ahmad?

That day, Marang went to the market to tell Ahmad the bad news. She could not stop her tears.

"Do not weep, dearest one." Ahmad comforted her. "I will take care of everything. Just be ready in your wedding dress when the time comes."

On her wedding day, Marang wore the beautiful pearls Ahmad had given her. Her eyes were misty with tears. Four strong guards marched into the wedding hall carrying the datu sitting on a golden throne. At his side strode the bridegroom dressed in a jeweled satin suit. Marang reluctantly looked up at his face and to her joy saw it was . . . Ahmad!

"Dear daughter," said her father, "Ahmad told me how much you love each other. His family has a fine reputation. I could not die peacefully if you

were unhappy, so I spoke to my friend and his son. They forgive me for breaking my promise. They give you their blessing."

Soon after the wedding the datu died. He was buried in his garden where a tree grew from his grave. It had leafy boughs and heart-shaped golden-yellow fruit. These were the first mangoes. People from all over the Philippines came to sit in the shade of the wondrous tree and taste its delicious fruit. The mangoes, they said, were a symbol of the kind datu's golden heart.

The Mean Datu

This is a folk tale from an island in the Sulu Sea near Mindanao. It tells about a datu who was known for his cruelty. Everyone feared him.

There are 12,000 kinds of plants in the Philippines. One of the most beautiful flowers there is the **waling-waling**, which Filipinos call "Queen of the Orchids." It grows in clusters on tree-trunks in the rainforests of Mindanao.

Bamboo and palms are used in many ways. **Nipa** huts, houses that stand on stilts, have a roof made of palm leaves (nipa), bamboo floors and walls. It is pleasant and cool to sit inside a nipa hut.

The datu had a beautiful, sweet daughter named Princess Bartuha. She didn't care about jewels and riches. She loved flowers and fell in love with a gardener who worked on the palace grounds. The young couple swore they would never marry anyone but each other. When the datu found out he was furious. He decided to get rid of the gardener and ordered his guards to kidnap him. That night, Princess Bartuha went for a stroll in the garden expecting to meet her beloved. She waited and waited but he did not come. Instead her father marched angrily to her shouting:

"You will never see him again!"

The princess covered her face with her hands and wept. She whispered a prayer. "Dear God, my heart is broken. Please change me into a flower! I will spread my perfume every night and my beloved will know I'm near."

The datu cried out in horror when he saw his daughter turn into a flowery plant. A lovely scent filled the air.

This flower still grows in the Philippines. At night, you can smell its soft perfume. Filipinos call it "Lady of the Night" or, in Spanish, "**Dama de Noche**." Its real name is **mirabilis**.

The Christmas Parol Festival

Christmas is the most important, most beloved, and longest holiday of the Philippines. It starts on December 16, instead of December 25, and ends on January 6. On the nine days before Christmas, mass is celebrated at the break of dawn "when the cock crows" (misa de gallo).

To say "Merry Christmas" like the Filipinos, stick colored paper letters on your window panes making the words: **Maligayang Pasko.**

Lights and Christmas go together. Bright colored lights, red ones, blue, green, or yellow twinkle in windows in the Philippines. They are **parol** . . . paper lanterns, often star-shaped, that light the way to mass. Starting in November everyone sells parol. You can buy them in stores, at stands, and from carabao-drawn carts. Long ago, Filipinos lit their Christmas lanterns with candles. Nowadays, parol hang in windows; lights from inside the house shine through them. Some parol even have their own electric bulbs.

Imagine how excited children must be to see almost every home in the Philippines decorated with glittering parol. Some people display their favorite parol long after Christmas ends.

The town of San Fernando near Manila is famous for its parol festival. The lanterns come in all shapes: stars, flowers, Christmas trees. Some parol are lit by more than 1,000 electric bulbs! Crowds line the streets waiting for the lantern parade. The parol turn as they pass by, their colors and patterns changing like giant kaleidoscopes. Some parol are so huge they have to be carried on a truck. The most spectacular parol wins a prize.

Men build the giant lanterns' wooden and wire frames. Women and children finish the parol, creating colorful designs out of cellophane, rice paper, paper garlands, and shells. They work in the traditional Filipino **bayanihan** spirit. **Bayanihan** is the spirit of cooperation. Each person helps and everyone cooperates. In the countryside, when Filipinos want to move, their friends help them carry their home to a new place.

The Spanish Arrive

Today, a bridge joins the important island, **Cebu,** to the neighboring island of **Mactan** where Lapu-Lapu defeated Magellan. Only bits of Magellan's cross still remain. They are protected inside a large cross displayed in the city of Cebu.

One evening Amambar, a Cebu chieftain, was walking on the beach. Suddenly, he saw a glittering cross so bright it dazzled him and he covered his eyes. He looked again, expecting the cross to be gone, but it was still there!

Puzzled, Amambar turned his head toward the sea. Five giant birds lay on the water. Men were walking on their backs! The men had white skins. Amambar was amazed. He had never seen such pale people before. They carried long, shiny swords at their sides. One man was dressed in a long black robe. He had a cross in his raised hand.

In a flash, the vision disappeared. Amambar died before the Portuguese explorer, Magellan, landed. He never found out that the huge "birds" were Magellan's ships and the white men his crew. The man in black was a priest.

In fact, in 1521, Ferdinand Magellan and his five ships reached the Philippines. The King of Spain sent him to explore and conquer new lands and to make the people Christians. Magellan was welcomed by local chieftains with traditional hospitality. He planted a wooden cross on Cebu Island, claiming the territory. Only Lapu-Lapu, the ruler of Mactan, wanted to fight the invaders. He and his warriors killed Magellan and forced the Spaniards to retreat. Only one of Magellan's ships, the **Victoria,** got back to Spain. It was the first ship to sail around the world!

Spain sent four more expeditions to conquer the Philippines. All failed. Finally, in 1564 the fifth succeeded.

The Spanish named the islands **Philippines,** after the Crown Prince, who later became King Philip II. They ruled the Philippines for the next 300 years. Filipinos lost many of their rights. A Spanish law forced them to take Spanish or Christian names. They earned little money and paid high taxes. All men between 18 and 60 had to work 40 days a year without pay for the Spaniards. They built churches, bridges, and large ships called galleons.

Galleons
Trading Across the Pacific

Galleons sailed from Manila to Acapulco (Mexico) with Filipino crews. They carried Chinese porcelain and silk, Spanish fans and clocks, Persian rugs, Indian jewels and cottons, Philippine pearls and pottery. Their voyages were long and dangerous. Ships often sank in typhoons. Sailors died of diseases. Still, it was good business for Spain. When the galleons returned safely they brought back silver worth 300 times more than the products they carried. Only Spanish merchants were allowed to own galleons. The galleon trade lasted more than 200 years.

Because of the galleon trade Mexicans and Filipinos share some of each other's plants, animals, words, and customs. Today you can find tobacco, cacao, and corn, all plants from Mexico, in the Philippines. Cattle, horses, and sheep arrived too. The words **chocolate**, **maiz** (corn), and **tomate** (tomato) came from Mexico. And so did **fiestas** (festivals)!

In Mexico, they grow mangoes, the large bananas, and the **ylang-ylang** flower, which all came from the Philippines. Mexicans know the words **tik-tik** (lizard) and **palay** (rice). Mexican women still use bright silk shawls, **mantónes de Manila**.

The Spanish used the Philippines mainly as a connecting point for their trade between Asia and Mexico. Filipino workers were poorly paid and worked long hours in the shipyards building the galleons. Many were forced to serve as sailors on long voyages. The galleon trade was extremely profitable for the Spanish.

Christmas Traditions

Filipinos usually call each other by nicknames. Almost everybody has one. Regina is **Revi**, Rosario is **Rori**, Carmen is **Menchu**, Salvador is **Dong or Doy**. Hardly anyone is called by a formal first name. Children always put **tiya** or **tita** (auntie) before a woman's name and **tiyo** or **tito** (uncle) before a man's name, even if they use a nickname. This is a sign of respect.

Filipino families are often large. Some grandparents have 35 or 40 grandchildren! They all get together on special occasions like Christmas. Some Filipinos who live in other countries come home to spend the holidays with their relatives. Relatives and friends welcome each other with a kiss on each cheek. Hosts shake hands with new guests and introduce them to everybody. Some children greet their elders in a special way, called **mano**. They might take a grandmother's or an uncle's hand and press it against their own forehead.

Families who have moved away from the Philippines keep some of their old Christmas traditions alive in their new homes. In the Philippines and in America, Filipinos hang parol, give each other presents, and eat all their favorite foods: **puto bumbong**, rice steamed in bamboo tubes and spread with fresh coconut and sugar; **bibingka**, rice cakes baked in clay ovens; **lechon**, roast suckling pig.

Filipinos who cannot get home for the holidays send **balikbayan** boxes full of special foods, clothes, and other presents to their families. It makes perfect sense to Filipinos, who live an ocean away from the islands in the United States, to share their good fortune with family and friends at "home." From North America to the Philippines, **balikbayan** boxes carry not only gifts but the Filipino spirit of sharing. Balikbayan means "return to the country."

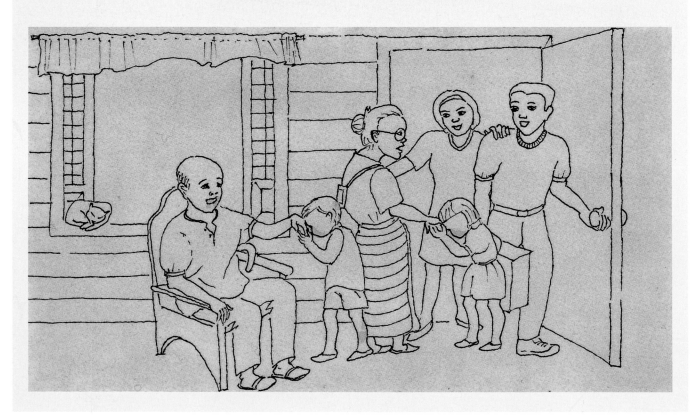

Making Parol

In the countryside, many children make their own parol. All you need is:

  10 long sticks (bamboo 1/8" x 1/2" x 36")
  5 short sticks (1/2" x 1/2" x 6")
  Yarn or tissue paper to make tassels
  Rice paper or tissue paper to wrap around stars
  Glue
  String (for hanging or carrying your parol)

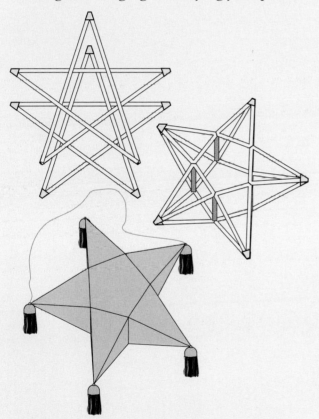

1. Form two 5-pointed stars with the long bamboo sticks.
2. Using the small sticks, glue the two stars together as in the illustration.
3. Cover the stars with rice paper.
4. Make tassels out of yarn or tissue paper strips.
5. Hang finished parol with string.

Bombones de Arroz

Filipinos enjoy Spanish dishes but change them to suit their own taste. When they make **sopa de fideos** (macaroni soup) they add **patis,** a sauce of fermented fish or shrimp. For **pastillas de leche** (milk bars) they prefer carabao milk. They put coconut milk in their **maiz** (corn) dishes. Here is the Filipino way to make Spanish rice cakes.

  1 cup soft boiled rice
  2 eggs
  6 tablespoons unsweetened coconut milk (you can buy it in cans)
  1/2 teaspoon salt
  1 cup all-purpose flour
  1 teaspoon vanilla
  1 teaspoon baking powder
  1/2 cup oil for frying

Mix the flour, baking powder, and salt, then add the eggs (well beaten). Add coconut milk and vanilla. Mix with soft boiled rice.

Heat oil in a big frying pan. Drop tablespoons of the mixture into the hot oil and fry until brown. Remove and put on a plate. *Cover the plate first with a paper towel to soak up the oil.* Serve with syrup or jam.

How the Pascua Plant Got Its Colors

A Folk Tale

Amor propio is very important for Filipinos. It means to behave in a way that makes others respect you, to feel you are a worthy person.

*The true name of the **pascua** plant is poinsettia, one of the plants that came from Mexico. It grows well in the Philippines. It is very popular, especially during the Christmas season.*

At Christmas time, Filipino children gather around their **lola** (grandmother) to hear the story about the **pascua** plant. She tells them about the little village boy from a poor family who walked every evening to church. There he admired the **belén**, nativity scene. He loved to look at the Virgin Mary in her blue cloak with silk stars, her husband, Joseph, the Holy Child in his crib, the angels, the shepherds, and the animals. But beneath the boy's joy was sadness, because he had no offering for the baby Jesus. He was embarrassed to come empty-handed while other children brought little gifts. His **amor propio** was hurt.

One Christmas, on the way to church, the boy noticed a plant with big, pretty leaves. "I'll pick a few branches," he thought, "and make a nice bunch for Baby Jesus and his Holy Mother."

He broke off a branch and, to his surprise, some of the leaves turned brilliant red, then gathered into the shape of a flower. He broke off another branch and the same thing happened again. Soon he had a beautiful bouquet of scarlet flowers and green leaves.

The happy boy ran to the church and placed his gift at the foot of Virgin Mary. At that moment, all the stars on her cloak began to twinkle. She lifted her hand and gently blessed the boy. Then a star appeared in the sky above the village and shone so brightly that the river looked like a ribbon of diamonds. As the boy walked back home, he saw that the plant whose branches he had taken was covered with scarlet flowers.

From that time on the pascua plant has been used for Christmas decorations.

Philippine Independence Day

Philippine Independence Day, marking its independence from Spain, is celebrated every year on June 12.

Flags decorate buildings and streets. In Manila, people lay wreaths of flowers at the monument of José Rizal. Families gather for picnics, games, and fireworks. There are parades and bands playing. It is Independence Day. Everyone will dance the **tinikling**, which means "dance of the herons." They skip in and out of two fast-moving bamboo poles. The air fills with the clicking rhythm of the bamboo poles clapping together, hitting each other, but never the dancers' quick feet!

In the United States, Filipinos celebrate Independence Day too. They may have a party and potluck dinner at their church or a big celebration for people from a whole region. There may be guests from the Philippines, raffles, and prizes. There's sure to be good food and good company, music and dancing.

In the Philippines, people visit each other and go to parties. Family members and helpers cook for days. They may set up big pots for cooking outside. The good smells float up and down the street. Some people peel, some chop, some fry, some boil, some clean up. Others decorate homes and yards with flags and paper garlands. Children run errands and help.

Doing things together in a pleasant way is called **pakikisama**. It means to get along and be friendly even in difficult moments, to cooperate. Pakikisama is an important Filipino value and helps people enjoy life in the Philippines.

The hostess usually doesn't know how many people will be coming to eat. Guests may bring along their friends and children. Surprisingly, no matter how many people come, there always seems to be plenty of food.

It is considered bad manners to rush to the table and eat. Guests usually help themselves only after they are asked several times. The hostess does not sit or eat until she is sure that everyone has taken enough food from the many dishes served. A Filipino saying is: *Always give your guest the best.*

One of the greatest Filipino heroes was José Rizal, a medical doctor and a writer, who wrote about the need for change in the Philippines. The Spanish accused him of stirring up armed rebellion and shot him on December 30, 1896. Today, December 30 is a public holiday in the Philippines. It is called Rizal Day. The place where Rizal was shot is a beautiful park in Manila.

Independence At Last

Lapu-Lapu, the first freedom fighter, was followed by thousands of others who spoke and fought for the rights of the Filipino people. Some became national heroes. Gabriela Silang, a young woman from the region of Ilocos, led a battle against the Spanish in 1763. Andres Bonifacio founded the secret revolutionary society, **Katipunan**, in 1892 to fight the Spanish. After his death, Emilio Aguinaldo took over as leader of Katipunan.

The contemporary Filipino flag (below on the right) has features from previous Katipunan flags (see flag on the left below). The three stars represent the three major island groups. Eight rays of the sun honor the first eight provinces that revolted against Spain.

Filipinos were unhappy under Spanish rule. The Spanish took their land, made them work without pay, and told them what they could and couldn't do. In the more than 300 years that Spain ruled the Philippines, Filipinos revolted 100 times! The Spanish finally caught, imprisoned, and killed most of the rebels.

Then, in 1898, Americans went to war with Spain. All over the Philippines, Filipinos joined the Americans in the battle against Spain. Their leader, Emilio Aguinaldo, proclaimed Philippine Independence on June 12, 1898. For the first time Filipinos flew their own flag and played their own national anthem. But they were not independent yet. The United States betrayed the Filipino fighters and took over the islands. Aguinaldo and his people still wanted an independent country and went to war with the United States. After several years of fighting, Filipinos had suffered devastating losses and the United States was in control.

Although the U.S. government was more interested in what the Philippines could do for America than in the well-being of Filipinos, the developments begun by Americans helped many Filipinos. Americans built roads and telephone systems. They brought better health care to the islands and opened many new schools. English became an everyday language.

During World War II, Japan invaded the Philippines. Filipinos, even children, and Americans fought side by side against the Japanese. The Japanese arrested, starved, tortured, and killed thousands. Finally, Americans and Filipinos led by General Douglas McArthur drove out the Japanese.

On July 4, 1946, Philippine Independence was proclaimed and accepted by the rest of the world. President Roxas said, *"Our independence is our pride and honor. We shall defend our nation with our lives and our fortunes."*

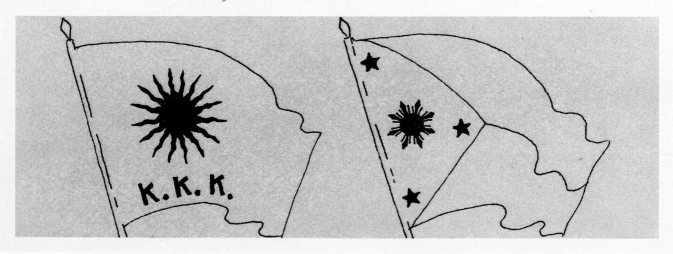

Chicken Adobo

This is one of the most popular dishes in the Philippines.

    1 chicken cut into 8 or 10 pieces
    1 crushed clove of garlic
    4 teaspoons soy sauce
    1/2 cup any kind of vinegar
    1 bay leaf
    1/2 teaspoon whole black pepper

Wash the chicken pieces. Put them in a pot that has a lid. Add the garlic, pepper, soy sauce, vinegar, and, bay leaf. Do *not* put the lid on the pot. Turn the heat to high. When the liquid starts to boil, turn down to medium heat and put the lid on the pot. Lift the lid from time to time and check how much liquid is left. When most of it is gone, poke the chicken with a fork. If it is tender, your dish is ready. If not, continue cooking a little longer. If necessary, add a little water to keep it from sticking.

When the chicken is tender, remove it from the pot. Place it in a pan and bake it in the oven for 30 minutes at 450 degrees. Wait for it to turn brown. Serve it with steamed rice. This is enough for 4 people.

Saba Fritters

There are 200 types of bananas in the Philippines. Cooking bananas are called sabas (or burros in the United States). Boiled saba are often sold on the street, for snacking. They are also used for this tasty dessert. If you can't find sabas, use plantain or plátano or you can use regular bananas. Don't boil them first, though. When buying sabas, choose ones which are yellow-brown-to-black, not green.

    4 sabas (plantains)
    1 cup flour
    1 tablespoon sugar
    1/2 teaspoon salt
    1 teaspoon baking powder
    1 egg, beaten
    1/2 cup milk
    1 cup cooking oil for frying
    1/2 cup powdered sugar

First, prepare sabas. Boil them in water (in their skins) until tender. Cool, peel and slice into 1/2 inch thick slices. Mix flour, sugar, salt, and baking powder. Add the egg and milk and mix just enough to blend. Add saba pieces. Heat the oil in a large frying pan. Drop in large spoonfuls of the mixture, fry one minute, turn over and fry another minute, or until brown. Lift out, drain on paper towels, dust with powdered sugar and serve.

Filipino Americans

Today, Filipino Americans are the second-largest group of Asian-Americans in the United States. California is home to the largest number, but many live in Hawaii, Illinois, New Jersey, New York, and Washington, D.C.

In the 1920s, when the Philippines were a U.S. territory, thousands of poor young Filipino men sailed to Hawaii and California. They worked 10 to 12 hours a day in fruit and vegetable fields. Some went to Alaska to fish for salmon. Many Americans feared the newcomers would take their jobs. Filipinos were treated badly. They faced racism, and laws that denied them citizenship and prevented their families from joining them. Lonely and homesick, some went back to their homeland. Most stayed in the United States to struggle for a better life. In the 1930s, Filipino farmworkers in California organized unions to fight for better working conditions. When Japan invaded the Philippines, Filipinos in the United States rushed to join the U.S. military. After the war's end, these soldiers, and later other immigrants, were allowed to become U.S. citizens.

In 1965, a new law let more Filipino immigrants enter the United States. Most of them were college educated: doctors, nurses, engineers, teachers, writers, and musicians. The United States needed their skills.

More than 2,000,000 Filipinos live in the United States today. They are from different islands and different backgrounds. They don't always speak the same Filipino language. But in the United States they come together to celebrate the things they have in common. They publish newspapers and magazines, have television shows and theater groups. They try to work together for a better life in America and for the people of the Philippines. They are part of America, but proud of their Philippine roots.

On Independence Day, many Filipinos wear their national costume. Women wear a dress, the **terno**, with butterfly sleeves and a long skirt. Filipinas love an airy material made of pineapple fiber called **piña**. The terno is often embroidered. It glitters with seed pearls, beads, and sequins.

The national costume of Filipino men is the **barong tagalog**, a long-sleeved, buttoned shirt, worn untucked without a tie. Dressy barong are often made of piña. They are embroidered all over, even on the collar, cuffs, and sleeves.

Filipino Music

There are many different musical instruments in the Philippines: the Moslem gong (kulintang), the two-string lute (**hagalong**), the fiddle with strings of human hair (**git-git**), the jaw harp (**kubing**), bamboo guitars, bamboo nose-flutes, and all kinds of drums. The **musikong bumbong** is a world-famous children's orchestra. The orchestra plays only bamboo instruments.

Today in the Philippines, most of the music you might hear on the radio is similar to what is played in the United States. When Filipino lyrics are put to Western music it is called "**pinoy** rock." Many Filipino musicians are looking for ways to combine their own traditional music with music from the West. They are trying to create a modern Filipino sound.

Pinoy is a term of endearment meaning Filipino. It is often used by Filipinos among themselves.

The Festival of the Higantes

This festival is held in the eastern province of Quezon, on August 19th.

Have you ever been to a giants' party? No? There is one in the town of Lucban. The **higantes** (giants) bow, turn, swing, and dance around a huge *toro* (bull). Firecrackers explode around the bull, popping and flashing with a long thunderous roar. Dark smoke hangs thick in the air. Children scream, cover their ears, and scramble away. Luckily, the giants and the bull aren't real. They are oversized puppets . . . 14-feet-tall puppets with people inside! The children aren't afraid, they are excited. They laugh, clap, and shout, dodging as the higantes come their way. The fun lasts all night.

The next morning, August 19, is the real festival day. A band plays loud music. Young women dress up as characters from Filipino myths and join the higantes in the street. The parade quiets as it approaches the church to be blessed by a priest.

Higantes are made of papier mâché fixed on bamboo frames. Men carry the giants on their shoulders. Higantes come in pairs: husband and wife, boyfriend and girlfriend, dressed in farmers' clothes. The males wear **camisa chino** (peasant shirts) and loose pants with red, green, blue, or yellow scarves tied around their necks. The females are dressed in **patadyong at kimona** (wide cotton skirts and thin blouses).

Filipinos in America have brought higantes to their communities too. Modeled after the higantes in the Philippines, these higantes appear at festivals and local events. They tower over the crowd, dipping and waving their arms. There are higantes of new and old Filipino heroes and giants from the revolution against Spain . . . José Rizal, Andres Bonifacio, and Emilio Aguinaldo. One higante wears the Philippine flag. With the huge figures to remind them, it is easy for adults and children to remember the heroes and patriots of their past.

When 19th-century Spanish landowners would only allow the people of Angono in Luzon one festival a year, the people created **higantes** to poke fun at their landlords. A famous higante festival is still held in the town in November.

How Kanlaon Killed the Dragon

This myth is about the hero Kanloan and a volcano on the island of Negros, in the Visayas. Filipinos say a dragon lived in its crater over 1,000 years ago.

There 56 volcanoes in the Philippines. 18 are active. Kanlaon is one of them. Volcanoes still erupt in the Philippines causing destruction and misery for the people.

One day a dragon appeared on the mountain. The monster was a mile long, had seven heads and seven mouths that spat flames, and 14 nostrils that blew black smoke. All the fields around the mountain dried up, straw houses burned, and frightened villagers fled. The King of Negros gathered his wise men.

"What can we do?" he asked.

"Send a messenger to the dragon to ask what he wants," they advised him.

The messenger was chosen, and trembling, he climbed halfway up the mountain. Too frightened to go on, he shouted the question. The dragon roared his reply.

"Tell your king I want to marry the princess!"

When the king heard the answer, he was heartbroken. He would have to sacrifice his dear daughter to save his people. As the princess was about to leave, a courtier rushed to the throne and fell at the king's feet.

"Wait!" he panted. "There is a young man at the palace gate ready to fight the dragon."

"If he saves my daughter," cried the king, "he may have all my gold, silver, and precious stones."

But the stranger didn't want gold or silver. He wanted to marry the princess. The king agreed. Any man was better than a dragon!

Now, no one knew the stranger was powerful Prince Kanlaon who spoke the languages of all the creatures on earth.

On his way up the mountain, Kanlaon met an ant. "Quick, go to your queen. Tell her, Kanlaon commands you to gather your army to fight the wicked dragon." The ant bowed and scuttled away.

Just then a bee flew by. Kanlaon stopped her and ordered, "Fly to your queen and say, 'Kanlaon orders your soldiers to fight the wicked dragon'."

"At your service," hummed the bee and buzzed away.

Then Kanlaon called to a huge eagle hovering overhead, "Fly to your king. Tell him that Kanlaon needs you to fight the dragon." The eagle nodded and vanished in the sky.

Kanlaon marched on. Millions of ants crawled at his side. A speck appeared in the sky. It grew larger and larger, buzzing louder and louder.

The bees had come! Soon the king of the eagles cut through a cloud, dove in front of Kanlaon, then carried him on his back to the mountain top.

There loomed the enormous dragon. He growled and twisted. Fire and smoke shot up in the air. The earth shook in the village below. People trembled. But Kanlaon was not afraid. He faced the dragon.

Ants crawled over the monster's paws, body, and tail. Bees flew into his eyes. The eagle pecked him with his powerful beak. The furious dragon swung blindly at Kanlaon. He missed. Again and again he attacked with his mighty claws. Kanlaon dodged and darted. He drew his silver sword and attacked the dragon. One after the other, he chopped off the dragon's seven heads. They fell into the deep crater and disappeared forever.

Kanlaon returned to the king's palace. The people clapped and cheered. He had saved them. The princess fell in love with the brave stranger and the king was relieved and happy to find he was Prince Kanlaon. The young couple was married the very next day. The wedding feast lasted seven days and seven nights. The whole village was invited.

If you visit Negros you can see the volcano where the evil dragon appeared. Can you guess its name? *Kanlaon!*

Everyday Heroes

Volcanoes aren't the only dragons Filipinos have to fight. Typhoons and earthquakes destroy towns and villages. Life in the Philippines is not easy. The people are still struggling to create a prosperous, strong, and unified country. Many people are very poor. Their children cannot get a good education. Jobs are hard to find. Thousands of Filipinos must leave the islands to work in other countries to help their families and look for a better life for themselves.

But when they visit the Philippines, they know they will always have a warm welcome. There is always a festival, somewhere, always something to celebrate! Filipinos have faced volcanoes, storms, and conquerors. They have a fighting spirit to meet today's challenges the way their heroes did in the past. They have islands that are still the paradise of legends. Whether they live in the Philippines, the United States, or another country, the descendants of Malakas and Maganda are courageous people, part of their islands, part of the Filipino family.

One of the loveliest Filipino words is "**Mabuhay**," a greeting that means "Welcome," "Good Luck," "Good-bye and Godspeed." It is the most important word to know when you visit the Philippines.

This isn't the end. In the Philippines or in your community, there is always another celebration. Until then . . . Mabuhay!

Laoag •

LUZON

Baguio
•

MANILA ★ Quezon City

VISAYAS

Bacolod
•
•
Iloilo

Cagayan De Oro
•

MINDANAO

• Zamboanga

Davao
•